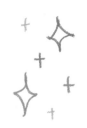

To my lovely niece, Matilde,
my first reader.

The Diver © Flying Eye Books 2018.

This is a first edition published in 2018 by Flying Eye Books,
an imprint of Nobrow Ltd. 27 Westgate Street, London E8 3RL.

Text and Illustrations © Veronica Carratello 2018.
Veronica Carratello has asserted her right under the Copyright,
Designs and Patents Act, 1988, to be identified as the
Author and Illustrator of this Work.

Published in the US by Nobrow (US) Inc.

Printed in Poland on FSC® certified paper.

ISBN: 978-1-911171-61-4

Order from www.flyingeyebooks.com

The Diver

by Veronica Carratello

Flying Eye Books

London | New York

In a little town in Italy, there lived a girl called Emma who dreamed of becoming a great diver.

When she LEAPT from the board, anything felt possible!

She trained hard every day,

and watched divers every night.

But things didn't always go to plan...

Walking home after training,
Emma was feeling low.

The big diving competition was in two days
and she wasn't ready!

But she picked it up anyway.

That night, as they all watched the divers on TV,
the little coin watched too.

In that moment, a dream blossomed in its tiny heart.
"I want to be a diver too!"

The bigger coins on the table just laughed...

...but all night, the little coin dreamed of diving.

Emma had no idea that this little coin had a dream of its own.

She gave it to the pizza delivery man as a tip,
but he thought it was too stingy.

She even tried to use it in the snack machine
at the swimming pool...

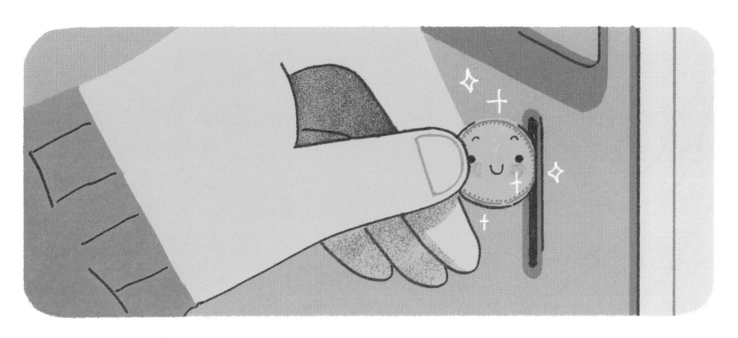

...but it wouldn't accept pennies.

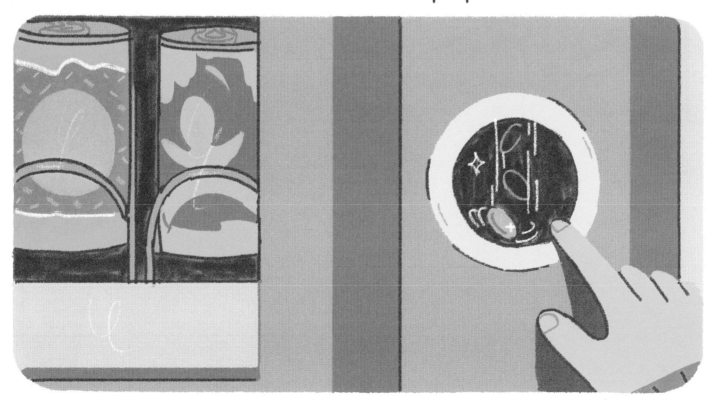

So she put it on the side and
joined her friends for their diving class.

The little penny couldn't believe its luck.

The penny watched the divers all afternoon,
and the more it watched, the more useless it felt.

There was no way it could be a diver.
It was a silly dream for a penny to have.

But Emma was worrying about her dream too.
The big diving competition was tomorrow morning!

So her dad told her an old story.

Squeezing the penny tightly in her hand,
Emma wished that she would win the diving competition.
But the penny coin also made a wish.

I want to be a diver!

And as she sent the coin spinning into the air...

...both of their wishes came true.